SHADES

DOING THE DOUBLE

Alan Durant

Evans

For Kit, top player, top son

Published by Evans Brothers Limited
2A Portman Mansions
Chiltern St
London W1U 6NR

© Evans Brothers Limited 2005

First published in 2005

British Library Cataloguing in Publication Data
Durant, Alan, 1958-
Doing the Double. - (Shades)
1. Young adult fiction
I. Title
823. 9'14 [J]

ISBN 0 237 52846 0

Series Editor: David Orme
Editor: Julia Moffatt
Designer: Rob Walster

DOING THE DOUBLE

He looked at me, pleading – my twin, my distorted reflection, the person I cared about most in the whole world, even when he'd done something stupid.

'You want me to do the double,' I said at last.

'Just for a couple of hours, that's all,' Dale said. He half smiled. 'Hey, who knows, you might even enjoy it.'

I doubted that very much. But, as usual, he'd won. When it came down to it, I couldn't say no.

Look out for other exciting stories
in the *Shades* series:

Prologue

Dale and I used to have this game we played. We called it Doing the Double. It was a football term we heard when we were kids. If a team wins the league and cup, then they do the double. But when *we* did the double, we pretended to be each other to trick people. Lots of twins do it. We hadn't done it for years and then it was only for a joke. But this time it was serious. Really serious. And I wasn't sure I could go through with it.

I was sitting in the changing room, just minutes away from taking the field for a County Cup semi-final and I was wondering what the hell I was doing there. I'd gone so cold there were goosebumps on my arms. Strangers kept coming up and clapping me on the back or patting my cheek.

'Hey, Dale, what's up? Don't tell me the iceman's got nerves,' said a tall black guy I'd never seen before. All I knew, from looking at his kit, was that he was the team's goalie. My team. No, *Dale's* team.

'I'm not Dale, I'm Joe,' I wanted to say – I should have said, but I couldn't. I'd promised Dale I'd do this for him and I couldn't back out now, however wrong it felt.

At that moment I hated football more than ever.

Chapter One

I hadn't always hated football. I used to love it like Dale still did. I guess it's not surprising that we loved football so much being the sons of a professional footballer – and not just any old footballer. Our dad was Nicky Green, one of the most talented players of his generation. That's what everyone always said about him anyway.

They usually said it with a sigh too, thinking about how he flushed all that talent down the toilet. I mean that literally too, with all the booze he drank. Nicky Green – famous footballer turned famous boozer.

When we were kids, we worshipped our dad – like just about every other kid did. Nicky Green was everyone's hero, no matter what team you supported. He was the cheeky chappy, the little guy with huge skills. He could run with the ball, pass and shoot with either foot, he had pace and balance, and bags of tricks. Backheels and nutmegs were his speciality. He made some of the best defenders look like club-footed monkeys. And he always did it with a grin. How could you help but love the guy?

Kids at school often used to ask us, 'What's it like to be Nicky Green's son?' Or they would say, 'It must be great to have

Nicky Green as your dad.' And in a way it
was. When we were small anyway. When
he was at the top of his game and the booze
hadn't kicked in and taken its toll. But in
another way it wasn't that great, because
we hardly ever saw him. If he wasn't
training or playing then he was promoting
some product or other – razors or energy
drinks or sportswear – or he was at some
starry event. His agent saw more of him
than we did, I reckon.

Sometimes I longed for a normal dad like
my friends had – one who would read us a
bedtime story, or take us to the park – play
football with us even. Dad didn't even do
that. He encouraged us all right, but he
never spent time with us, passing on his
skills. I guess both Dale and I were
naturals. We learnt a lot from playing with
each other. Each of us tried to get one step

ahead of the other, which wasn't easy, as we knew each other's moves so well. A lot of the time we even shared the same thoughts. Well, we did back then. These days I don't really know where Dale's coming from half the time – and no doubt he'd say the same about me.

It seems weird to say it, but the best times were when Dad was injured. Then he'd be around the house for a while and he'd do some of the stuff that other dads did. A minor injury – a slight strain or pull – was the best news anyone could bring. Anything more major, though, was really bad news. It was when he got his first major injury, a broken left leg, that he started drinking. He just got so bored and frustrated. He loved playing football more than anything in the world. More than his sons, more than Mum. Football really was his life. Take that away and he was like a fish with no water.

People say now, 'It must have been terrible for you when your dad was doing all that drinking.' But it wasn't – well, not at first. We didn't really notice. Dad wasn't violent. He didn't shout or swear. We just saw less and less of him. He used to stay out night after night, and when he was at home, he'd fall asleep a lot. Sometimes he'd drop off halfway through saying a sentence. Dale and I thought it was funny. We'd do impersonations of him, and laugh ourselves silly.

But then the drinking got worse. It affected his playing. It started to make the newspaper headlines. Kids at school who'd worshipped him, now sneered and said nasty things about him. Dale and I regularly got into fights about it. We would take anyone on – it didn't matter how big they were. I suppose the difference was that I knew when to stop, when the odds were just too heavy against us – Dale never did. And he's the same now. Trouble seems to sniff around him like a dog on heat. Trouble like going out on the town two days before an important County Cup semi-final – the most important match of his life – having too many drinks and ending up crocking his ankle trying to jump a fence for a stupid dare. Trouble like that. And I'm the one who has to pick up the pieces.

Chapter Two

'No,' I said. 'No way. I'm not doing it. This is your mess. You get yourself out of it.'

'Come on Joe,' Dale pleaded. 'You know there's nothing I can do. My ankle's like a football. No way can I play in two days' time. I wouldn't be asking you if I had any other choice. You know that.'

'I know you're an idiot,' I said bitterly.

'What's the saying, "Like father like son"?'

'It was an accident, Joe. Anyone can have an accident,' Dale reasoned.

'Yeah but you were drunk,' I said. 'Not everyone goes out drinking with their mates a couple of days before an important football match. Only idiots do that.'

Dale put on this sulky face, like I'd really wronged him. It was a look I'd seen lots of times since we were kids. If you accused him of something, even if he'd done it – like now – he'd try to make you feel bad. It was his way of turning defence into attack, I suppose. It wasn't going to get him anywhere this time, though.

'Look, if you really don't want to help...' he began.

I cut him off.

'I'm not doing it, Dale,' I said, shaking my head.

I thought about what it was Dale had just asked me to do: to take his place in his team, Blackstock Youth, for the semi-final – and worse, to pretend that I was him. He'd missed training a lot lately and his coach, Bob Smith, had given him a final warning: if he stepped out of line one more time he'd be out of the team. Getting an injury a couple of days before the semi-final would be the final straw. Smithy would bring in one of the reserves to replace Dale and if the team won the game, then it would be the replacement who'd play in the final, not Dale. And Dale really wanted to play in that final. He'd been told there would be academy scouts there from a few different clubs – some Premiership ones among them.

I shrugged.

'Anyway, I don't play football, you know that.'

'You used to be really good,' Dale said. 'You were as good as me.' He considered that for a moment. 'Well, nearly.'

'Yeah, well, that was ages ago,' I said.

Dale was right. I used to be good at football. Dale and I were the stars of our team. We played as strikers – twin strikers. One season we banged in a hundred goals between us, which was a league record. I loved playing back then. But I hadn't kicked a ball now for nearly two years – not since the day Dad walked out on us to live with his new woman. He turned his back on us; I turned my back on football. Basketball was my game these days.

Dale sighed.

'Look, Joe, I'm not asking you to do anything amazing. Just run out there and don't make a complete fool of yourself, that's all. You're fit, you know how to play.

I'm not asking a lot.'

'Dale, I hate football,' I said. 'You know that and you know why.'

'Yeah, 'cos of Dad,' he said. ''Cos Dad betrayed you. Don't you think it's time you got over that, Joe?' Dale had never taken against Dad for what he'd done. He'd kept in regular contact, was always going round to see him. I guess that's because they were so alike. I hadn't spoken to Dad at all since he left.

'Besides this has got nothing to do with Dad,' Dale went on. 'It's me who's asking, not him.'

He looked at me, pleading – my twin, my distorted reflection, the person I cared about most in the whole world, even when he'd done something stupid.

'You want me to do the double,' I said at last.

'Just for a couple of hours, that's all,' Dale said. He half-smiled. 'Hey, who knows, you might even enjoy it.'

I doubted that very much. But, as usual, he'd won. When it came down to it, I couldn't say no.

Chapter Three

When I was a kid, my favourite video wasn't a Walt Disney cartoon or the *Simpsons*. No, it was *Nicky Green's Golden Goals*. I used to watch it over and over: Nicky Green's mazy run from the halfway line and dribble round the helpless Everton goalie; Nicky Green's last-minute flying header that knocked Spurs out of the FA

Cup; Nick Green's amazing bicycle kick against Porto in the Champions League Quarter Final… I knew each of those fifty goals inside out. Dad used to laugh about it. He joked that I'd watched his moves so much that I could be a spy for one of his opponents.

'I bet you could tell them how to stop me,' he said.

'No one can stop you,' I told him. But I was wrong about that. There was one person who could stop him – and had: Dad himself.

I was thinking about that, as I tied the laces on my boots for about the fifth time before taking the field for the County Cup semi-final. I wondered suddenly what Dad had been like at my age. Like Dale probably, I reckoned. He'd have been bouncing about the changing room, joking with everyone, playing tricks – not nervous at all. I was so nervous I could barely do my laces up. My hands were all shaky. I felt sick and light-headed. I just wanted this to be all over.

'OK, lads, time to get out there and do your stuff.' Smithy was giving his final pep talk. 'I want to see one hundred percent effort from the start. Don't let them settle. Understood?'

There was a murmur of assent and the players started to make their way out onto the pitch. I was at the back. Smithy stopped me.

'You're very quiet today, Dale,' he said. 'Are you all right?'

'Yeah, fine,' I muttered.

'Good. I want to see some real commitment out there. No switching off when the ball's not at your feet.' I nodded.

'And don't forget – pass the ball. You're not a one-man team.'

'Yeah,' I muttered again. Then I turned and ran out. My head was spinning. So, Dale was lazy and didn't like to pass. Well, nothing had changed there then.

Today, though, Dale was going to be different.

Chapter Four

Blackstock's opponents were Merton Athletic. No one knew that much about them because they played in a different league. They'd won it, though, Smithy had told us that much, just as Blackstock had won their league. Both teams were trying to do the double ... just as I was.

I was playing up front, of course, where

Dale usually played. Our skipper, Carl, won the toss and chose to kick off. Dale had told me about him. He said he was all right, but he liked to shout a lot, and he'd let you know if you'd done something wrong – as I was soon to find out.

'OK, Dale,' he said to me as he jogged by. 'Same play as always.'

'Right,' I nodded. But I didn't have a clue what he meant. It made me feel even more nervous. My heart was beating like crazy as I stood next to the ball, ready to kick off. My fellow striker, Danny ('nice but useless', according to Dale) bounced up and down beside me, eager to get started.

The ref looked at his watch. Time seemed to stand still. He put the whistle to his lips.

Peep!

I froze. Danny nodded at the ball.

'Dale?' he said.

'When you're ready, son,' said the ref sharply.

I tapped the ball forward. In a flash the ball was back at the feet of Carl. He took one pace forward and booted the ball upfield … straight to the Merton left-back, who controlled it and booted it forward – and out of play.

Carl glared at me.

'What you doing, Dale?' he shouted angrily.

Obviously I was supposed to run into the space occupied by the Merton left-back after taking the kickoff.

'Sorry,' I said, cursing Dale for not telling me this important detail of how his team played. I felt a right fool.

I made a few mistakes in the early stages. I wasn't used to such a physical game – if you touched anyone in basketball you gave away a foul. I'd forgotten that football is quite different. The tackling was really tough – quite apart from all the nudges, pushes, shoves and barges, some of which the ref saw, but not all. For the first ten minutes or more I couldn't get on the ball at all. Every time it came near me, I had it whipped off my foot or head by a Merton defender.

'Come on, Dale!' Carl hissed at me after I'd lost the ball for about the tenth time. *He* was everywhere – chasing, tackling, running, passing. I felt tired just watching him.

At last I got a break. Carl fed a pass through to me and for once I reached the ball before my marker. I flicked it past him, turned and ran. My football skills might have been a bit rusty, but one thing I did have was pace. I left the defender standing and was away running towards goal.

I might have got a shot in too, if the left-back hadn't stepped across and chopped me down. Still, at least, it gave us a free kick in a dangerous position. It got me a nod of approval from the skipper too.

'Top turn, Dale mate,' he remarked as he stepped up to place the ball for the kick. Unfortunately, he blasted his shot over the bar.

So maybe it wasn't just me who was nervous.

Chapter Five

At half-time the score was still nil-nil. Neither side had really made any clear-cut chances, but our goalie (who I'd discovered was called Kola) had made one brilliant save to keep out a long range shot from Merton's best player.

I hadn't had a great match but at least I'd got to know the names of a few more of

my team-mates – and found out a bit about
how they played.

'You all right, Dale?' Danny asked me
as we were walking to the touchline to get
our drinks. 'You seem, I don't know, well,
not yourself.'

He didn't know how right he was.

'I'm fine,' I said. Then found myself
having to repeat the same thing to Smithy
a few minutes later when he was giving us
his half-time talk. I thought maybe he'd
take me off – and I'd have been quite
happy if he had. I'd done my bit for Dale by
showing up. I was ready to step back now.
This wasn't my team after all.

Smithy didn't sub me though.

'Bit more effort, Dale,' was all he said.

I felt a lot more at ease starting the
second half than I had the first. I guess I'd
got used to the pace of the game and my

touch had started to come back. Like I said before, Dale and I were naturals really. Football came pretty easily to us. We'd been playing since we were babies. In fact Mum used to say that she reckoned we started playing before we were born, we kicked so much inside her!

In the first minute I set up a chance for Danny from which he nearly scored. He should have too. I flicked the ball into space beyond the last defender and Danny only had the keeper to beat. But he hit his shot straight at him.

'Unlucky,' I said.

But it seemed a lot worse than that when, from the keeper's clearance, Merton Athletic took the lead. A punt downfield, a missed header by our centre back, and the Merton striker was in. He didn't make Danny's mistake. The ball was rocketing past Kola before he had the chance to move. 1-0 to Merton Athletic.

We had it all to do.

Chapter Six

I felt different now. The Merton goal suddenly made me feel a lot more committed and serious. I thought, *If we lose this, then Dale won't be playing in the final.* I felt somehow like I'd have let him down – which was crazy really. I was doing him a favour after all.

Anyway, it was like I'd had a shot of

adrenalin straight to the heart. I was full of energy all of a sudden. I pulled my marker from one side of the pitch to the other as I went in search of the ball. Carl certainly noticed the difference.

'Nice work, Dale,' he said after one of my runs had won us a corner.

Carl took the kick himself. An in-swinger from the left that dipped beautifully right in the middle of the goal where I was running in to meet it. I jumped, neck tensed to nod the ball in the net, when, thump! Something banged into me and knocked me to the floor. *That's got to be a penalty*, I thought – till I saw Danny lying next to me.

'Sorry, Dale man,' he said as we got to our feet. 'I thought it was going over your head.'

'It's OK,' I shrugged.

Smithy wasn't so forgiving though. Next time the ball went out, he pulled Danny off. He sent on a sub, a skinny Asian kid called Wakim, who looked like he'd fall over if the wind blew too hard.

'Push right up, Dale,' the coach ordered. 'Let Wakim do the running.'

I raised my hand to gesture that I'd heard. I just hoped he knew what he was doing.

Chapter Seven

Wakim may have been small and thin, but man could he run! I thought I was quick, but Wakim was a two-legged greyhound. He didn't have a great touch on the ball, but he had pace to burn. He'd only been on the pitch a moment or two when he got his first chance to run. A quick throw down the wing and Wakim was away. He was far too quick for the Merton defenders. All they could do was block him out and give away a free-kick.

Time was running out and we were getting a bit desperate now. The kick was just to the left of the area about twenty-five yards out – my distance. Well, it used to be. Carl placed the ball and prepared to take the kick. I jogged over to him.

'What you doing, Dale?' he asked. 'Get in the box.'

'Let me take it,' I said simply.

'What, you going to take a shot from here?' he said in disbelief.

'Sure,' I said. 'I've scored from there before.'

'When?' Carl muttered.

'Well, a while ago,' I admitted. I didn't add that "a while" was over two years!

The ref blew his whistle.

'Come on, lads,' he called. 'It's your time

you're wasting.'

Carl looked in my eyes. I don't know if he was impressed by what he saw there or wasn't feeling that confident after his poor free kick in the first half, but he nodded.

'Don't waste it,' he muttered, then ran away towards the penalty area.

I took a couple of steps back. I had this picture in my head for an instant of one of those golden goals in that video of Dad's that I used to watch. Nicky Green's unstoppable curler against West Ham United. I ran forward, wrapped my foot around the ball as I kicked it. I couldn't have hit it any better. The ball curled round the two-man wall and zipped towards the near corner of the net. The keeper dived, but too late and the ball was going away from him all the time. It smacked against the inside of the post and pinged over the line.

'*Goal!*'

We'd equalised and I'd scored.

I just stood there grinning. I must have looked really stupid. Not that any of the Blackstock players cared. In seconds, half the team had run over to where I was standing and jumped on me. Their congratulations and laughter rang in my ears.

We were back in the match.

Chapter Eight

We were into the last ten minutes and it was still anyone's game. We had most of the pressure but Merton were still looking dangerous on the counter.

I was completely caught up in the match now. I hadn't wanted to play and I'd happily have come off at half-time, but now I was hooked. I wasn't just playing for

Dale, I was playing for me. I wanted to win this match. I guess I'd forgotten how much fun playing football is. I loved playing basketball, but it'd never given me the buzz I was feeling at this moment.

Wakim and I set up Carl for a chance, but his shot went wide. He was mad with himself. Now it was my turn to encourage him.

'Bad luck, skipper,' I said. 'Keep going.'

I thought from his expression that he was going to give me a mouthful. But then I realised he wasn't angry, he was puzzled. I guessed Dale didn't say things like that.

Kola made another fine save to foil Merton's goalscorer, palming a powerful shot over the bar. I started to run back for the corner, but Smithy shouted at me to stay where I was.

'Keep moving those defenders around,' he called.

To be honest, I was getting a bit tired. I wasn't used to running round for this long – and a basketball court is nowhere near as big as a football pitch. Still, I did my best to follow Smithy's instructions.

The corner was cleared easily. The ball fell to Wakim halfway inside our half – and I knew what was coming. So did all the Merton players but there wasn't a lot they could do about it. Once he'd got the ball under control, Wakim was off, spindly legs flying as he sprinted into the Merton half. I knew what I had to do. Tired as I was, I gave it everything as I raced to try to keep up with the speedy sub. Luckily, he got held up briefly by the Merton right back who pushed him out wide. But he couldn't stop him.

I knew a cross would come and I had to get into the centre to meet it. I ran so hard, I thought my lungs were going to burst. But my efforts paid off. When Wakim reached the by-line and pulled the ball back I was there in the centre of the goal to meet it. I lunged forward with head and hand and the ball hit me and span past the keeper into the net.

'Goal!' The joyful shout went up again. I heard the ref's whistle blow and turned to see him point to the centre spot. My teammates rushed towards me in congratulation once more. But this time I held up my hands to push them away.

I ran to the ref.

'Well played, son,' he said. 'Nice header.'

I shook my head.

'I didn't head it,' I said. 'The ball came off my hand. It wasn't a goal.'

The ref looked at me like he thought maybe I was kidding him.

'Are you sure?' he said.

I nodded.

'It was handball,' I confessed.

'Well that's very sporting of you,' he said. 'From where I was standing it looked like you'd headed it.'

He blew his whistle again and pointed back towards the Merton Athletic goal.

'Free kick to Merton,' he said. 'Handball.'

Nobody could believe it.

Carl gaped at me like I'd suddenly turned into an alien.

Smithy shouted something that would have made his mother blush.

The rest of my team-mates groaned and grimaced.

A lone voice called out in appreciation of my action.

'Well done, Joe!' it praised.

My heart did a sudden flip as I glanced towards the touchline. He was standing, half-hidden behind Smithy. (How the hell hadn't I spotted him? How long had he been there?)

For the first time in nearly two years, I was looking at Dad.

Chapter Nine

I don't know how I managed to get
through those last minutes. My legs had
gone to jelly, my head was on fire, I could
barely breathe. I staggered around in a daze
until the whistle blew to end my turmoil.
Thankfully, there was no extra time. It had
been agreed that if the match was drawn,
there'd be a replay the next weekend. If it

was still a draw at the end of that, then there'd be extra time and penalties. But not today. I couldn't have played anymore anyway. I'd given everything.

As I walked off, the other players ignored me. Smithy was waiting on the touchline to have a go at me.

'What were you doing out there, Dale?' he fumed. 'You let the referee make the decisions, that's what he's there for.'

'It was handball,' was all I could say. My mind was spinning all over the place.

'Let him be,' said a familiar voice. It was Dad. 'He did the right thing. Cheating's for losers.'

I couldn't help myself.

'Yeah, well, you should know,' I muttered. I wasn't thinking about football. Dad had always played fair – he'd never been a diver or anything. I was thinking how he'd cheated on Mum and on me.

'Who's this, Dale?' Smithy demanded. Then his eyes widened with sudden recognition. 'Nicky Green,' he said. 'You're Nicky Green.'

'Yeah,' Dad said. 'But this isn't Dale. This is Joe.'

Smithy was overwhelmed. He stood there, looking from Dad to me, his face the picture of bewilderment.

'So it was you who called "Joe",' he uttered eventually. 'I wondered what that was all about. I'm still wondering…'

'Dale's my twin brother,' I said, adding, as if it would make any sense at all to the dumbfounded manager, 'I was doing the double.'

'I think you'd better explain,' said Dad.

So, haltingly, I told them the whole story.

Chapter Nine

Smithy and Dad had a chat when I'd finished and they decided there was only one thing to do. We all three went off to find the Merton Athletic manager. He'd just finished his after-match analysis and was sending his players home.

'Can we have a word?' Smithy said, smiling uneasily.

'Yeah, sure,' said the Merton manager. But he wasn't looking at Smithy; he was looking at Dad. It's not every day you're face to face with a football legend.

'Good to see you, Nicky,' he said in a kind of matey but awed manner.

'Yeah. Good to see you too, Deano,' Dad said. Now it was my turn to look surprised: they knew each other!

'Deano played for QPR,' Dad explained. 'Marked me out of the game once.'

'Once,' Deano repeated. He smiled. 'Didn't get near you the other times. It's good to see you looking so well, Nicky. I know things have been tough.'

'Yeah,' Dad said simply. It was true too, he did look well – much leaner and fitter than when I'd last seen him. He'd lost that bloated, red-faced, kind of bleary look he'd had when he was drinking. It looked like he'd given up the bottle at last.

Dad gestured at me.

'This is my son, Joe,' he said.

Deano nodded.

'A chip off the old block, eh?' he said. He held out his hand to shake.

'Nice goal, son,' he said. 'And an even nicer bit of sportsmanship. Your dad's obviously brought you up the right way.'

Dad shuffled uncomfortably.

'Thanks,' I mumbled, feeling uncomfortable too.

There was an awkward silence. Then Smithy came to the rescue.

'We've got something to confess,' he said. 'It's about Joe here.' He told Deano about me doing the double to help Dale out. He told him everything.

Deano listened, nodding now and then. He looked serious.

'Well, strictly speaking, I should report this to the League,' he said. 'Playing an unregistered player is a disqualifying offence.'

'Yeah. I know,' said Smithy grimly. 'I didn't know anything about all this till just now, but, like they say, ignorance is no excuse. We've committed an offence, whether we knew it or not.'

Deano gave me a searching look.

'You got anything to say, son?' he said.

I felt awful, really awful. I didn't know what to say. I was just doing Dale a favour; I'd never thought that this might happen, that I'd get the whole team thrown out of the cup, because I'd played.

'I'm sorry. I really am,' I muttered miserably.

'He and his brother are very close,' Dad said in my defence. 'They'd do anything for each other – always have.'

'Yeah, I see,' said Deano. He stood in silence for a moment or two, considering. 'Well, look, I'll tell you what,' he said. 'That was a very good game out there, Joe, and but for your honesty, your team would have won. Now, because of your, well, dishonesty your team could lose. I reckon that balances out. And no harm's been done. The match was drawn, we start again next week on equal terms. I don't see any necessity to take this any further.' He gave me another searching look. 'And I reckon you've learnt your lesson.'

'Yeah,' I said. I was just so relieved that I hadn't ruined everything, that things could still be put right for Dale and his team. Well it felt like *my* team too now.

Deano's face softened into a smile. He turned to Smithy.

'I'll tell you something else – you better

register this boy quick, before I nab him!'

Smithy laughed and so did Dad. Then he put his arm round my shoulder. It was a small gesture but it felt like the most important touch I'd ever had. It felt good, really good. My eyes were welling up. I'd missed Dad so much.

'We'd better tell Dale the good news,' he said.

I nodded, too choked up to speak. I seemed to have been through just about every single emotion in the past couple of hours. But right now I was feeling so happy I felt like crying.

I had a dad again.

Chapter Ten

Dale and I both played in the replay. It was like old times. We had such an amazing understanding even though we hadn't played together for two years. He knew when and where I was going to make a run, whether I was going to pass or shoot, and I was the same. And Dad was there watching, encouraging. During the week, he and Mum had talked in a friendly way for the first time in ages. OK, they weren't going to get back together and Dad wasn't coming back home, but at least we were all talking to one another. We were a family once more.

Dale and I both scored in the replay. Blackstock Youth won 3-1. Two weeks later we did it again in the final to help Blackstock win the cup. We'd already won the league, so now we'd done the double – really done the double, no tricks, no pretending.

At the end of the match, Dale gave me a high five.

'You're the best, Joe!' he said. 'If I've got to walk around my whole life with a double, I'm glad it's you.'

'Yeah, well, you're not so bad,' I replied. I grinned. 'Most of the time.'

Dale grinned back.

'We make a great partnership, don't we?' he said.

'Yeah,' I agreed. 'It's good to be back.' And it was, it really was.

After the final, we were approached by a few scouts inviting us to try out for their clubs' academies. Dad spoke to them. He's going to help us decide what to do, which one to choose. He's already phoned to ask about facilities and what they do to look after young players properly. He doesn't want what happened to him to happen to us, he says.

It seems like having a famous footballer for a dad might not be such a bad thing after all.

Look out for this exciting story
in the *Shades* series:

FIGHTING BACK

Helen Bird

It was a cold night. Freezing fog pooled
round the orange street lights, forming
giant traffic cones along the street. Amita
had been glad to get to bed. Her father had
eventually shut up about Cath, but it had
been a difficult evening.

She found it hard to sleep. All the
experiences of the day went round and
round in her head. Would Southampton
work out for all of them? Could her father
really settle down after what had happened
to the shop?

She heard voices outside in the street. Loud, drunk voices, laughing and singing. For a moment, Amita felt a rising terror. She started to shake with fear. Plucking up courage, she slipped out of bed and peered out of the window. Two young men were winding their way down the street. She could see their football scarves quite clearly as they passed under the lights.

She forced herself to calm down. They were harmless. She was being silly. It couldn't happen here!

Suddenly she heard doors banging inside the house, and her father yelling.

'Call the police! We need help! Javin! Call the police I say!'

Amita pulled on her dressing gown and rushed out of her room. Her father's bedroom was at the front of the house too. He must have been woken by noises outside.

He was cowering at the top of the stairs. Rajeeb was arriving, with Uncle Javin close behind. Amita pushed forward. Her brother was hopeless in situations like this.

'Dad, Dad. It's OK. There's nothing wrong. It was just two men walking past, that's all.'

'It won't happen here, Gayan,' said Javin. 'This is a respectable neighbourhood. They don't do things like that.'

But Gayan wouldn't be reassured.

'I saw them. I heard them. Football hooligans, louts. Screaming and laughing.'

Amita tried to take control of the situation.

'Rajeeb, go and make tea for us all. I'll stay with Dad.'

She gently pushed her father back into his room and shut the door.

'Dad. Listen to me. It was bad luck

before. They built the new football stadium and the shop was on the way to the station. It could have happened to anyone.'

'But it happened to *us*. It was the end of everything!'

'I know that, but we're here now and we can make a new start.'

'Not while there are racist louts around.'

'It's quiet again now. It was just some young men coming home. There's nothing to worry about. We're safe here.'

The tea arrived, and the family sat drinking it together. Gayan felt ashamed, but he just couldn't help himself. He knew Amita was right, but that only made it worse. He had looked foolish in front of his brother and his children. Javin was a success, he was a failure. Even as a father.

Blitz - David Orme
It's World War II and Martin has been evacuated to the country. He hates it so much, he runs back home to London. But home isn't where it used to be…

Gateway from Hell - John Banks
Lisa and her friends are determined to stop the new road being built. Especially as it means digging up Mott Hill. Because something ancient lies beneath the hill. Something dangerous - something *deadly*…

Hunter's Moon - John Townsend
Neil loves working as a gamekeeper. But something very strange is going on in the woods… What is the meaning of the message Neil receives? And why should he beware the Hunter's Moon?

A Murder of Crows - Penny Bates
Ben is new to the country, and when he makes friends with a lonely crow, finds himself being bullied. Now the bullies want him to hurt his

only friend. But they have reckoned without the power of crow law…

Nightmare Park - Philip Preece

Dreamland… a place where your dreams come true.

Ben thinks it's a joke at first. But he'd give anything to be popular. Losing a few short minutes of his life seems a small price to pay.

Plague - David Orme

Plague has come to the city of London. For Henry Harper, life will never be the same. His father is dead, and his family have fled. Henry must find a way to escape from the city he loves, before he, too, is struck down…

Space Explorers - David Johnson

Sammi and Zak have been stranded on a strange planet, surrounded by deadly spear plants. Luckily mysterious horned-creatures rescue them. Now all they need to do is get back to their ship…

Tears of a Friend - Joanna Kenrick

Cassie and Claire have been friends for ever. Cassie thinks nothing will ever split them apart. But then, the unthinkable happens. They have a row, and now Cassie feels so alone. What can she do to mend a friendship? Or has she lost Claire … for good?

Treachery by Night - Ann Ruffell

Glencoe, 1692
Conn longs to be a brave warrior, just like his cousin Jamie. But what kind of warrior has a withered arm?

Who Cares? - Helen Bird

Tara hates her life – till she meets Liam, and things start looking up. Only, Liam doesn't approve of Tara taking drugs. But Tara won't listen. She can handle it. Or can she?